D0193243

Contents

The First Order

Many years ago, the evil Empire
ruled the galaxy. The Empire was
harsh and cruel, and the people
of the galaxy wanted to be free.

A brave rebellion began.
After many hard battles,
the rebels freed the galaxy!

The rebels didn't know that
some members of the Empire
had escaped. These Imperials
traveled to the far side of the
galaxy and named themselves
the First Order.

Ever since then, the First Order
has been planning its revenge.

First Order commanders

Supreme Leader Snoke is in charge of the First Order. Snoke is very mysterious and keeps himself hidden. He relies on three commanders who control the First Order for him.

Kylo Ren is the greatest warrior in the First Order. He uses a lightsaber to defeat his enemies.

General Hux is very smart.
He is in charge of the
First Order's army.
Hux is building the
First Order's new secret
weapon, the Starkiller.

Captain Phasma
leads the First Order's
soldiers, known as
stormtroopers.
She is brave
in battle,
but cruel.

The Resistance

Princess Leia was one of the
rebels who defeated the Empire.
She never believed that the
Empire was gone forever.

Leia created a group called the
Resistance, who would watch for
signs that evil had returned.

Many brave pilots and soldiers
have joined the Resistance.
They want to protect the galaxy.

The Resistance has built a
secret base where its members
spy on the First Order.
Leia wants to know what the
First Order is planning to do.

The village

Poe Dameron is Leia's best pilot. Leia gives Poe a top-secret mission. He must fly to the planet Jakku and meet an adventurer named Lor San Tekka. Lor has secret information that can help the Resistance.

Poe lands on Jakku with his loyal droid, BB-8. Jakku is a hot, dry desert. It is not a place where most people would want to live.

Lor San Tekka lives in a village in the wilderness. Poe finds him, and Lor gives Poe a special object. The object has the information hidden inside it.

Invasion

The First Order has attacked
Jakku! Stormtoopers have come
to the village looking for Lor
San Tekka and his secret object.

The villagers try
to fight, but there
are too many
stormtroopers!
They have
to surrender.

Poe gives the object to BB-8. The little droid manages to get away, but Poe is captured. Oh no!

Finn escapes

FN-2187 is a stormtrooper.
He realizes that the First Order
is evil, and he doesn't want
to be part of it anymore.
He wants to run away.

FN-2187 rescues Poe, and they
escape together. Poe thinks
that FN-2187 is a silly name,
so he renames his new friend
Finn. That's much better!

Poe and Finn steal a TIE fighter and try to fly away, but their ship gets shot down and crashes on Jakku. Finn parachutes to safety, but when he lands he finds that Poe has vanished.

Rey

Jakku was once a battlefield in the war against the Empire. There are wrecked starships scattered across the planet. Many scavengers have come to Jakku to take what they can from the wreckage.

This girl is one of those scavengers. Her name is Rey. She has lived alone on Jakku for many years. Rey was left on the planet as a child, and she doesn't remember her family.

Rey in the junkyard

Rey is very good at scavenging. She always finds valuable bits of technology. She takes them to Niima Outpost, which is the biggest town on Jakku.

At Niima Outpost Rey trades what she finds for food, but it is never enough and she is always hungry!

Rey is a genius with machinery.
She has built herself a speeder
out of spare pieces of junk.

Rescuing BB-8

Rey is relaxing and eating some food when she hears frightened beeping. It's BB-8! He is being kidnapped by another scavenger.

Even though Rey doesn't know BB-8, she leaps into action and rescues him. Good job, Rey!

BB-8 wants to stay with Rey,
but Rey offers to take him to
Niima Outpost instead.

Unkar Plutt

Rey's boss is a mean junk dealer named Unkar Plutt. Unkar controls all of the food in Niima Outpost.

If the scavengers that work for Unkar can't find anything to trade, then they go hungry.

When Rey arrives at Niima, Unkar tries to buy BB-8 from her. Rey says no, and Unkar sends his gang of thugs after them. Luckily, Rey knows how to defend herself.

Niima Outpost

After his TIE fighter crashes, Finn has to walk through the hot Jakku desert. Eventually he reaches Niima Outpost. Rey and BB-8 have defeated Unkar's thugs, but First Order stormtroopers are coming after them!

Rey and BB-8 run into Finn as they try to get away. They decide to join forces and escape together.

They need a ship to escape on. Rey finds a rusty old freighter underneath a tarp. It is called the *Millennium Falcon.*

Battle above Jakku

Rey, Finn, and BB-8 take off in the *Millennium Falcon*, but First Order ships chase after them!

Rey is a great pilot. She manages to outfly the First Order pilots.

Finn gets into the gunner
position and tries to destroy
the enemy ships.

Together they escape from Jakku,
but then the *Millennium Falcon*
breaks down.

Han and Chewbacca

Han and his copilot, Chewbacca, are smugglers. Han used to own the *Millennium Falcon*.

The two smugglers are traveling in a huge star freighter. They come across their old ship broken down in space. They are very happy to have the *Millennium Falcon* back!

Han and Chewie are very famous. They helped the rebels win their war against the Empire. Rey and Finn are shocked when they realize who Han and Chewie are.

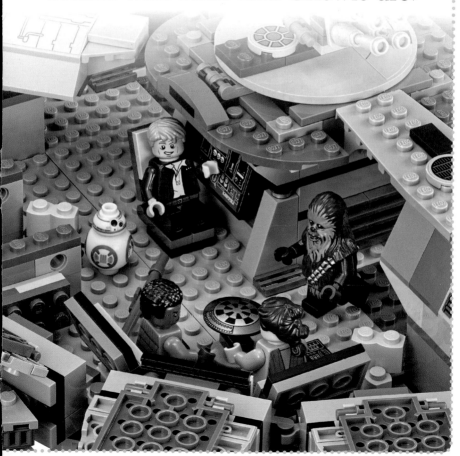

Gangsters

Han and Chewie have made
a lot of enemies over the years.
One of these enemies is a gang of
pirates known as the Kanjiklub.

The Kanjiklub is a scruffy
group of thieves and bandits.
They are led by a fierce
warrior named Tasu Leech.

The Kanjiklub attack Han and Chewie's freighter, but Han, Chewie, Rey, Finn, and BB-8 all escape in the *Millennium Falcon*.

Rey is captured!

The band of brave heroes travel to visit an old friend of Han and Chewie's. Her name is Maz. She is one of the most famous smugglers in the galaxy.

Unfortunately, the First Order has tracked the heroes to Maz's castle.

An army of stormtroopers
lands to try to capture them.
There is a big battle, but Poe
and the Resistance arrive and
save the day! The stormtroopers
retreat, but they capture Rey
and take her away.

The Resistance base

Han, Chewie, Finn, and BB-8 travel to the Resistance's secret base. They have learned that the First Order has built a giant weapon called the Starkiller on an icy planet. This is where Rey is being held prisoner.

At their base the Resistance puts together a plan to rescue Rey and destroy the Starkiller.

Han, Chewie, and Finn will sneak into the First Order base while Poe and his brave Resistance pilots attack from above.

The Starkiller

Han, Finn, and Chewie land
on the Starkiller base in the
Millennium Falcon. At the same
time, Rey escapes from her
prison cell. They all find each
other inside the base.

They find out that there is a problem. The Resistance's X-wings can't shoot through the Starkiller's thick armor. What are they going to do?

Battle in the base

The stormtroopers protecting the Starkiller wear special armor to keep themselves warm. They are called snowtroopers.

The door into the Starkiller is locked and guarded. Finn and Rey need to find a way to open it.

While Han and Chewie defeat the troopers guarding the door, Rey finds the box that controls it.

Rey is able to open the door, and Han and Chewie rush inside. They place their explosives and then Chewie sets them off.

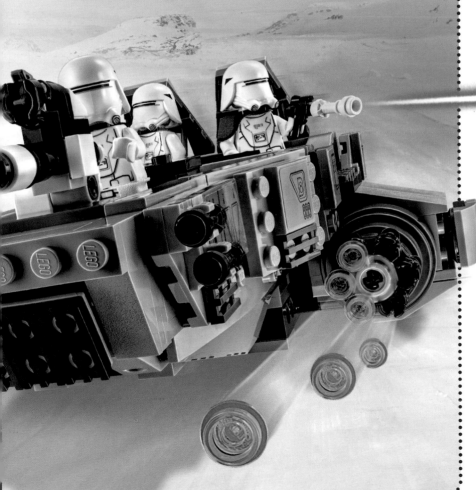

Poe into action

In the sky above the Starkiller, a big battle is raging. The X-wings of the Resistance are battling the TIE fighters of the First Order.

When Chewie sets off his explosives, it makes a hole in the Starkiller's armor.

Poe sees his chance! He fires into the hole and soon the Starkiller is badly damaged. It starts to tear itself apart.

Kylo's revenge

Kylo Ren is very angry. He storms
out into the snow looking for
Finn and Rey. Kylo doesn't
know that Finn and Rey are
stronger than he thinks.

Finn and Rey battle Kylo Ren. It looks like Kylo is going to win, but then something amazing happens. He is defeated!

General Hux uses a shuttle to rescue Kylo, while Finn and Rey are picked up by Chewie in the *Millennium Falcon*. The Starkiller blows up as they fly to safety.

The Starkiller has been destroyed. The Resistance has won the battle, but the war is only beginning!

Quiz

1. What is the name of the First Order's Supreme Leader?

2. Who created the Resistance?

3. What is the name of Poe's droid?

4. Which planet does Rey live on?

5. Which ship do Rey and Finn use to escape from Jakku?

6. Who is Han Solo's copilot?

7. What is the name of the First Order's secret weapon?

8. What are the First Order's cold-weather soldiers known as?

Answers:
1. Snoke 2. Princess Leia 3. BB-8 4. Jakku 5. The Millennium Falcon 6. Chewbacca 7. The Starkiller 8. Snowtroopers

Written and Edited by David Fentiman
Project Editor Eleanor Rose
Designer Jenny Edwards
Senior Designer Owen Bennett
Pre-Production Producer Marc Staples
Senior Producer Lloyd Robertson
Managing Editor Paula Regan
Design Manager Guy Harvey
Creative Manager Sarah Harland
Art Director Lisa Lanzarini
Publisher Julie Ferris
Publishing Director Simon Beecroft

Dorling Kindersley would like to thank Randi Sørensen, Paul Hansford,
and Martin Leighton Lindhardt at the LEGO Group.

For Lucasfilm
Senior Editor Jennifer Heddle
Art Director Troy Alders
Story Group Leland Chee, Pablo Hidalgo, and Rayne Roberts

First American Edition, 2016
Published in the United States by DK Publishing
345 Hudson Street, New York, New York 10014
DK, a Division of Penguin Random House LLC

Page design copyright © 2016 Dorling Kindersley Limited

001–299995–Aug/16

LEGO, the LEGO logo, the Brick and Knob configurations and the Minifigure
are trademarks of the LEGO Group. © 2016 The LEGO Group. All rights reserved.
Produced by Dorling Kindersley under license from the LEGO Group.

© & TM 2016 LUCASFILM LTD.

All rights reserved.
Without limiting the rights under the copyright reserved above, no part of this publication may be
reproduced, stored in or introduced into a retrieval system, or transmitted, in any form, or by any means
(electronic, mechanical, photocopying, recording, or otherwise), without the prior written
permission of the copyright owner.

A catalog record for this book is available from the Library of Congress.

ISBN 978-5-0010-1436-2

Printed and bound in China

www.LEGO.com
www.starwars.com
www.dk.com

A WORLD OF IDEAS:
SEE ALL THERE IS TO KNOW